The Kicho
The Dolls of Society Series, Volume 1

Victoria L. Szulc

Copyright © 2017, 2022 Victoria L. Schultz/Hen Publishing, a Hen Companies Brand

All rights reserved. Although there are references to actual historic events, places, and people, all of the characters, places, and dialogue in this book and its related stories, are fictitious, and any resemblance to any person living, dead, or undead is coincidental.

A gentle word to my readers/trigger warning: *although my pieces are works of fiction, my books and stories contain scenes and depictions that may upset certain audiences.*

Cover illustration/photo: Victoria L. Szulc

Cover Design: Michele Berhorst

Model: Stephanie Biernbaum

ISBN-13: 978-1-958760-11-6

FOR ALL THOSE WHO LOVE THEIR DOLLS

They hold our wildest dreams, keep our deepest secrets, and are our best friends when we are lonely.

ACKNOWLEDGMENTS

Special thanks to the St. Louis Ball Jointed Doll Group for the knowledge and inspiration.

London, 1852

"Can I see it, grandfather?" A small voice piped up beneath the sturdy oak workbench.

"Patience, dumpling, patience." The elderly gentleman tinkered with a very special doll. The toy's wooden limbs rolled between his fingers as he placed brass fittings over its ball joints. With deft turns of the last screw, he closed a hidden panel and held up the gift for his only descendant. Chika would be the recipient of all his worldly possessions upon his death, even if she wasn't of his blood.

"Wow! She's pretty." The petite Japanese girl gazed at the doll. "She looks like me!"

"Yes, Chika, she does." The grandfather, Mr. Jacob Wadsfellow, admired his handiwork. He'd taken care in securing a ceramic face that was molded with the slanted eyes of Asian folk. Jacob had gone to great lengths in finding suitable hair, hardwood, and fabric for the doll as well. He placed an ornate blue embroidered robe on the doll that was as beautiful as the child he'd adopted.

"Now, before I let you look at her, you must promise me," Jacob put his goggles aside, stooped down in front of Chika, and hid the gift behind his back.

"Yes, grandfather." Chika clasped her hands in excitement.

"Do not lose your dolly. Ever. Understood?"

"Yes!" She squealed as if she would burst.

"In Japanese, she is 'kicho,' which means precious. Let's name her."

"Aika!"

"Yes, Aika is a strong name. Take very good care of her. She's as precious as you." He handed over the doll as Chika's eyes widened. "Look her over. Every piece of her was made just for you. Give her a little shake."

Chika did as asked, and a gentle tapping emitted from inside the doll.

"Hear that? It's her heart."

"Yes. She has a heart!"

"Of course she does. Just like you. A very special one at that, because this heart is a crown coin. And it's been blessed to help protect you." Jacob knelt next to the girl to show her the doll's most important secret. "If I should leave or if you need help, you press the brass button here. Inside is the coin, yes?"

"Yes, grandfather."

"You take it to Mr. Yoshito's shop and give him the coin. He will help you, no matter what the circumstance. You promise?"

"Yes, I promise." Chika ran her fingers along the silken locks of the doll. "But grandfather, what happens if she's taken?"

"Hmm, well, let me tell you a story." As Jacob stood, his creaky knees reminded him why he needed to have the doll finished. He was close to eighty years old. Time was of the essence.

He shuffled to his favorite rocking chair and motioned for Chika to sit on his lap. "Long ago, dollies like yours were gifts to protect their owners. If given to the wrong person, the scared spirit of the doll would remind the thief that she did not belong to them."

"And if they did not give her back?"

"The dolls would come alive and kill those who dared to steal them." Jacob chuckled.

"Really?"

"Yes, well, the wisdom of the ancient ones tells us not to steal. Again, remember Chika, do not lose your dolly." He squeezed the child in a warm hug and hoped that he would live long enough for her to fend for herself. Chika's mother could not.

Hong Kong, 1847

"Ugh, this place. Horrific." Amaya wrinkled her nose in disgust. She leaned against the separating table in the backroom of a laundry. The piles of smelly clothing seemed to grow even after hours of endless washing. The putrid linens made her stomach churn. She continued to conceal the vomiting that resulted from morning sickness. She had no idea how she was going to hide her pregnancy and continue to work under such revolting conditions.

Amaya spied at the doorway that led to the cobbled streets of Hong Kong, then listened to the front of the laundry. It seemed busy enough that she could escape out the back for a moment. She ran out into the near dark, braced against the outer wall of the laundry, and let her bile fly into an ash pit. A scared cat hissed and shot away through the cluttered alley. Her shirt and apron were soaked from the humidity of the laundry. She gathered an edge of her apron to wipe her equally sweaty brow. *Why was life so unfair?* Her mind fogged over.

Blocks away, Jacob Wadsfellow hurried along as quickly as he could. The carriage he'd hired wouldn't go further into the slums. He had to find the lost daughter of a fallen princess before the warring factions of the Chinese would fight over Hong Kong. It was his last foreign mission from the Society to do so. Months of searching had led him here.

Jacob had inherited his father's cobbler business. It was a shop that had long been a part of a large network of underground spies, the Society, which worked for the greater good. His trade made him comfortable with those who worked for the East Indies Trading Company. His English looks of pale pink skin and grey hair hid his knowledge of Asian ways and customs.

The young woman he intended to collect, Amaya, was in danger, of that he was certain. Her background, however, was questionable.

Jacob had reviewed her history again before this latest search. Amaya's parents, Ming and Chin, had been linked to Japanese royalty and each spiritually gifted with visions. But favor with the Emperor was lost. Ming became pregnant around the age of sixteen. Rumors abounded that Chin had been Chinese. The two escaped to Hong Kong. It was easier to hide in a large city teeming with trade. Or so they thought. Shortly before their daughter Amaya's birth, Chin dreamt that the samurai had come for them. Once Amaya arrived, she was sent to a convent and granted protection from the Society. Ming and Chin vanished into the American Wild West never to be seen again.

"Such a tragedy to be without motherly love," Jacob muttered as he caught his breath in the darkness. "And to have such need of help."

Amaya was a curious child and gifted like her parents. However, her inquisitive personality proved to be her downfall. Early in her adolescence, she escaped the convent and found comfort in the tawdry opium dens that quieted her gifts. A visiting missionary was sent out to reclaim Amaya. Instead, he was captured by Amaya's beauty and impregnated her.

"Fool." Jacob cursed the Member who had put his charge into such danger. "Hopefully, I'm not too late."

Amaya returned to the slums, worked whatever jobs she could find, stole opium, and wondered how she was going to handle a child on her own. These very thoughts continued to cloud Amaya's mind as Jacob approached her at the laundry.

"Hello, Miss." Jacob's voice startled the young woman.

"If you have laundry, you can drop it off in the front." Amaya stood tall even though she was lightheaded. She reminded herself that she needed to be careful. *Who knows who the convent would try to send?*

"Are you Amaya?" Jacob could see the worry in her eyes.

"Who wants to know?" She tried to sneer, but it came out in a whimper.

"My name is Jacob Wadsfellow—"

"Are you with the convent?" Amaya braced to run even though her stomach was flip-flopping again.

"No, but I am here to help you."

"I—I don't need any help." Bile and more of the fruit she'd tried to eat crept into her throat.

The laundry manager burst into the alley. "Amaya? You lazy girl! Outside again? I'll cut your pay. And who is this man?"

Despite her best efforts to combat her nausea, Amaya

vomited again but this time it splattered all over the manager's expensive leather shoes.

"Ah, no pay! None. This is a disaster. You go and never come back!" The manager spat and slammed the door behind him, leaving the elder Englishman and the wayward young Japanese woman alone in the dark alley.

"Change your mind?" Jacob teased.

"Okay, I'll go with you. But if we end up anywhere near the convent, I'll run." Amaya smirked.

Hours later, Amaya was fast asleep on a plush bed in an expensive hotel in Hong Kong, her belly filled with nourishment. In the adjoining room, Jacob messaged his superiors about their impending trip to London. At last, he had found the young woman that many had been searching for. He'd even usurped the missionary who'd seduced Amaya.

That young man, Brother Evan, wasn't clergy. He'd infiltrated the convent and had planned on taking Amaya to London himself, but for much more seedy needs of an opposing underworld faction.

London, 1848, Seven Months Later

"How do you feel today, Amaya?" Jacob kindly asked his charge while he repaired an expensive boot for a wealthy businessman.

"About ready to pop." Amaya had mastered English to the point where she was developing a British accent. She shifted uneasily in her chair as she repaired an embroidered handkerchief. She didn't like to work, but at least it kept her mind off the impending birth.

"But you were able to eat well this morning? The doctor says it should be about a week, yes?" Jacob peeked at her while he continued to stitch a swatch of unruly leather. Physically, Amaya had been well, it was her mind he'd worried about. Although his work through the cobbler's shop was important, Amaya was his primary concern.

"Yes, on both accounts."

"Good, very good. I want you to be completely satisfied with, well, everything. You are to tell me if you need anything. Remember what we talked about?"

"Yes, sir, if I should feel any labor pains to call for you immediately."

"Good girl." Jacob crossed the room and kissed her forehead. Taking care of Amaya had been a challenge. She was restless and bored during the day. But at night, he overheard her dreams. She spoke of worlds unknown, prophecies, and royal peoples, all with her eyes closed. He hoped that once her child was born, the distraction of pregnancy would be gone, and Dr. Arav would be able to tap into her mysterious mental gifts.

"Why don't I make you tea, and maybe you'd like to take an afternoon nap?"

"That would be delightful!" Amaya faked a smile.

"Very well, then. I'll be back shortly." Jacob promised as Amaya gazed out the window to a sunny London afternoon.

"Hopefully, I'll never be back." She mumbled to herself. "I've escaped before."

Hong Kong, 1844

The clanging bells of the chapel tower woke Amaya as they had done her whole life. On most days they were an intrusion of good slumber. But on others, the church bells were a reprieve from frightening night terrors. They were so real that Amaya would awake screaming while sweating and tearing through her bedsheets. She did not realize that she'd been gifted with prophecies that came to her in sleeping states.

These episodes had earned Amaya a special assistant, Sister Bethany, and her own quarters, far away from the other orphans of the convent.

On this morning, Amaya remembered a sweet yet powerful dream. There was a girl, much like herself, that had a wonderful doll. The girl spun round and round with her toy. As she swirled, her kimono grew with a kaleidoscope of vibrant colors. Dragons and tigers leaped from the sleeves and danced merrily with them. A sweet song of flutes accompanied the creatures. Everything stopped; the girl stared at Amaya and whispered "Kicho". A warmth filled Amaya. She felt like the girl in the dream knew her. Maybe it was her mother?

Amaya's happiness became a burning disappointment as she remembered the absence of her parents. When she questioned Sister Bethany, the good nun told Amaya that she'd been abandoned, but at the convent, she would be loved and appreciated.

And indeed, she was. All the children in the orphanage wing were given good food and education. But some, like Amaya, had special help, a minder one could say, that assisted with additional needs. Amaya was taught Japanese and Mandarin, in addition to proper English. Unlike other girls, Amaya was allowed to play with the boys, at least until she hit puberty. It was then that she began to have nightmares. Amaya was separated from the others.

This built a resentment that Amaya couldn't understand. At first, she blamed the other children.

"Sister Bethany, I don't understand why they can't think like me. Or play like I do. I mean, doesn't everyone have dreams?" Amaya pouted after the other girls bullied her.

Sister Bethany hugged her charge. "Everyone is blessed differently by God. And Amaya, my dear, you are very, very special."

And then she wondered aloud about her parents.

"Sister Bethany, whatever happened to my mum and daddy?"

"Amaya, you precious soul. We've spoken about this, remember? Your parents were in an accident of sorts." Sister Bethany cooed and held her close. "We're your family now. We have everything you need here."

But finally, she began to blame the sisters that had taken her in. Weeks before this day, Amaya and Bethany were studying in the library.

"Sister Bethany, when may I go outside the convent? I mean, other children my age have taken small trips. Surely, I will too?"

"Yes, dear. In due time. You're just not ready yet." A concerned look crossed the sister's face.

"I would like to see the flowers we've studied. And the birds and the other animals."

"Again, Amaya, you must have patience. When you are older, you will travel to far places. You're just not ready yet. Understood?"

Amaya felt a surge of anger in her gut. She was mad enough that on that very night after bedtime was called, she slipped out the rose trellis from her window, shimmied over the convent fence, and walked out in the nighttime air of Hong Kong.

She was instantly enthralled by the streetlamps, the homes painted in brilliant colors, and the cacophony of people, carts, and animals in the streets. Amaya bounced from block to block, peering into shop windows and stalls at exquisite furnishings, beautiful dresses, and a toy store filled with incredible dolls.

As it grew late, painted ladies hopped into carriages with well-dressed and not so well-behaved men. The sellers of fruits and nuts closed their carts for the night. Beggars asked her for money if she could spare it. It was then that Amaya realized she was only in a grey woolen dressing gown. No wonder people had eyed her suspiciously.

She continued to an immense park. There were ominous statues and gates at the perimeter. Amaya slid between the large bars of a closed gate and wandered in. A full blue moon lit the grounds. She wondered at the hoots of owls and the elegant swans that made a last glide across an indigo-colored lake. A warm breeze carried the smell of pastries from a bakery on the other side of the park.

Amaya followed the smell, left the park, and found the enchanting shop. The window was filled with colorful buns, sponge cakes, and egg tarts. She ignored the closed sign and tried the front door. Finding it locked, Amaya persisted and went to the side of the shop. Surprisingly, an alley door was open. She crept down into a cellar. After her eyes adjusted to the darkness, Amaya saw light at the top of another set of stairs. She crept like a cat and peered through the lock. The shop had been emptied but a sole lamp illuminated the room.

Amaya twisted the knob and stole into the bakery's kitchen. A kitten emitted a pleasant meow, rubbed against her legs, and scurried away. The smell of pastries was enchanting. Amaya lifted the cloths of the platters and could not resist sampling the shop's wares.

The fruit-filled buns melted in her mouth. The red and blue berries stained her lips and chin as she greedily ate at least one of each variety. Once sated, she went out the way she came. Amaya smartly remembered the street names and landmarks. Soon she was in front of the toy store again, only this time the streets were empty. A gaslamp cast a golden glow on the dolls in the window. *If I could only have one*, she thought.

Amaya dared not try the front door and went around to the side. Unfortunately, this entrance was locked. As she dejectedly moved away, she passed an ash pit and thought she saw a petite hand sticking out. Amaya squatted down, gently tugged at the wooden limb, and pulled out a mockup doll. It was made completely of wood, with all its pieces intact, a tuft of brown hair, and a painted face. Amaya shivered as she tucked it into her gown.

Amaya grew tired as she stumbled back to the convent. Climbing the outer fence and the trellis to her room was much harder than when she exited. She tumbled into bed and fell asleep within moments.

"Amaya! Wake up, dear!" Sister Bethany shoved her

charge. "Didn't you hear the bells? And good heavens, what is this mess?"

Amaya's eyes focused as she awoke. Her tongue instinctively ran along her sticky lips.

"Look at yourself! Your nightdress is filthy. Are those fruit stains? Did you get a snack after hours? And where did this come from?" Sister Bethany yanked the sample doll from Amaya's arms.

"I-I don't know." Amaya stammered. In her sleepy state, she was almost believable.

Sister Bethany cooled her temper and sat on the bed. "Tell me, child, did you have a dream last night? A night terror?"

"Yes." It would be the first of many lies that Amaya would tell in order to savor the outside world. "I got scared."

Sister Bethany sighed. She knew of Amaya's nightmares. It was only two months ago that Amaya finally stopped wetting the bed and sleepwalking. With puberty nigh, it was going to take a supreme effort to protect Amaya. Prior experience showed that visionaries often grew their talents into adulthood. The sisters were counting on sharpening her skills. But Amaya would need to survive adolescence first. "Alright then. Just for today, I will bring you breakfast. Tidy up."

Sister Bethany's stomach fluttered as she kissed Amaya's forehead. Her gut had never lied to her before, but she had a feeling that Amaya would be in trouble.

Amaya waited several weeks until her next adventure. She attended her classes and studied hard to cover her plans. The second time she'd gone, Amaya figured out how far she could go to see parts of Hong Kong and then get back in time to not be sleepy.

The Kicho

Within a month, Amaya would leave every night. She kept a satchel of extra clothing and boots under her bed. Sometimes she would take off for just minutes, other times for hours. She picked through trash for trinkets to trade from paperboys and stole from sleepy imbibed beggars. She listened to buskers and the sounds of merriment from the English trading pubs. The fruits, nuts, and savory buns she stole from lowly vendors warmed her heart and filled her belly. She learned to move quickly and not get caught.

Amaya kept the old wooden doll as her talisman. The weight of it bouncing in her satchel made her feel safe.

After seeing the exciting sights of the city, she became bored with the strict convent and its stoic way of life. Her vivid dreams embarrassed and scared her. Amaya saw people in danger, strange machines, and places she'd only heard about in books.

For about two years, Amaya's activities eluded the nuns. But one particular night after her sixteenth birthday, Amaya had a night terror of a city she'd never been to. Of London in peril, of green gases filling the skies and explosions rocking the ground beneath her. She awoke soaked in sweat. Out of habit, she threw on her hidden clothing and sneaked into the city. Her footsteps echoed from block to block while she sought someone or something that would shut out her horrific vision. A cunning voice from an alley made her stop.

"You look lost." A thin Chinese man stood in the doorway of a tony-looking British pub.

"I'm not." Amaya raised her chin and prepared to walk away.

"But you're running? Yes? Would you like to rest for a moment?" He lifted his bowler. "And should you not have time, I could give you a taste that you'll want to come back for?"

Amaya paused. She knew she'd been very lucky in not getting caught either in or out of the convent. But a gleam in the man's eye told her that he did have a special treat. "Alright then, what do you have?"

"Try this. If you like it, you can have more on one condition. You tell no one where you got it from unless they have money for it." He proffered a small package from his waistcoat. "Put out your hand."

Amaya did as he asked while the stranger lifted a corner of the brown wrap and poured a pinch of powder into her palm. "Taste it."

Amaya licked the mysterious acrid powder. She closed her eyes at the delicious warmth that spread through her body.

"Now, come inside and sit." He tugged at her coat sleeve. Amaya was drawn into a plush darkened room with elegant people languishing over chairs and loungers. A thin layer of fog gave them the semblance of ghosts enjoying a quiet evening at home. "Here, relax." The last thing Amaya remembered of that evening was that she'd felt better than she had in a very long time.

"Get up! Silly girl. We clean, get out!" Amaya was startled awake by a petite Asian lady poking her with a broom. "And pull down your skirt! No one needs to see those knickers!"

Amaya threw her clothes together and stumbled into daylight. Her head and between her legs ached. A wave of nausea came over her and vomit soon splattered the alley. She scurried back to the convent only to find Sister Bethany waiting for her as she crawled through the bedroom window.

"Oh, Amaya...what have you done?" Sister Bethany cried.

"I-I don't know. I feel sick." Amaya collapsed onto the bed in a heap of sobs.

"Alright, now. Let's get you cleaned up. You can stay in bed today; we'll get you fresh nightclothes." The good sister noticed a white film around the wayward teen's mouth but gasped as she helped Amaya with her underclothes. Small stains of blood ruined her bottoms. "Um, it's alright child. You're just having your menses, right?" The nun was lying to herself as she clothed the poor soul. It was clear that Amaya had been violated. "Rest dear. I'll bring up food."

Amaya couldn't completely rest as the nightmares came back. She wanted more of that mysterious powder to make them go away. And so began a vicious cycle of Amaya escaping, finding opium, coming back to the convent, and Sister Bethany caring for her. Within weeks Amaya started to disappear for days at a time. The nuns realized they could no longer manage her by themselves and called upon superiors to send help.

Aid arrived in the form of Brother Evan. He was a tall, slender fellow, with cropped brown hair, deep brown eyes, and pale skin. To the Society, he was a clever young man that could charm the socks, and well...other things off women. It wasn't long before he found Amaya in one of Hong Kong's seedier opium dens. With a little money, one of the bartenders helped the Brother move Amaya into a carriage. At first, Brother Evan delivered her to a safe house where she could sober up.

On the first morning, he watched her awake and then instinctively grab for her satchel.

"You're not going to find it." Brother Evan reprimanded. "I have food for you. And shelter."

"I can get all those things myself." Amaya snapped, jumped off the bed, and crashed onto the floor of a spare bedroom.

"Now, now. Patience dear. We must proceed slowly." He lifted her onto the bed with a grin.

Amaya felt something she'd never had before. Her heart melted with the strength of the Brother's arms. As he covered her with a blanket, Amaya surrendered but not without a last challenge.

"I will stay with you on one condition—I want you to tell me what happened to my parents. The real story. Not a candy-colored dream invented by one of the sisters." Amaya sneered.

"Alright. I will find out. It may take some doing, but you'll need to trust me. Understood?"

"Yes. I will." Amaya fell asleep as she relented to Brother Evan's demands. She would give more to him than she'd ever planned.

Within a week, Amaya had kicked her addiction and her nightmares came back, more terrifying than ever. Evan stayed beside her, cooing and wooing. After a couple of weeks, he romanced her, breaking all of his supposed solemn vows, and began to share her bed.

Amaya was smitten. She'd never loved before, and Brother Evan made her feel safe. One morning he brought in a full breakfast and fed her. "Good morning. Today, I fulfill a promise. I'll take you to a person who knows about your parents. But you must hide in the carriage. You can't be seen. Agreed?"

"Yes!" Amaya leaned in for a tender kiss. "Can we go now?"

"Finish your breakfast. And then—" he held her chin in his hand. "We find out."

In the next hour, Amaya was blindfolded and seated next to Evan in a small carriage. Finally, the clatter of the horses' hooves stopped. "Say nothing, not a word. I will lead you in."

Amaya trembled with excitement as Evan grasped her hand. She heard the creaking of a door as she was led in. It closed behind her as he whisked the scarf from her head.

Amaya was instantly devastated. She was back at the convent. "Welcome home, Amaya."

"What? No, no, no. You promised. You told me!" Amaya crumpled to the floor. Brother Evan dashed away without a word.

Sister Bethany whispered in her ear as she helped her up. "This is for the best. Come. It will be alright."

Amaya's head spun as she was taken back to her old room. She would leave again; of that she was certain.

As Brother Evan slid away from the convent he was racked with guilt. He would come back later to collect his pay. By then, Amaya was already spirited away to a much older gentleman who would prepare her for adulthood without mixing business with pleasure.

London, 1848

Amaya drew another deep breath as she crept out the back door of Jacob's shop. It was long after midnight, and London's famous fog was filtering into the city streets.

Slithering down the steps had taken every inch of strength and patience. She knew exactly which steps creaked, what floorboards moaned, and the precise amount of noise that would wake Jacob. *Old fool*, she thought.

For months she'd played along, listened to his fanciful stories and adventures that sounded more like the boasts of an old man. At night she pretended to sleep and babbled the most outrageous gibberish that she could think of. Jacob claimed he could help her with her visions. Amaya didn't believe him.

No one would ever know what she saw in her dreams unless they'd offered her the world. Being cared for by a curmudgeon cobbler was not enough, even though Jacob had cared for her like his own child. The silly fool had even made her a doll and named it Fumi, which meant history. She didn't need any of his possessions, wisdom, or kindness. She just wanted the opium that allowed her to rest and made her visions go away.

Amaya made it outside without waking Jacob. Once out into the damp eve of London, Amaya didn't even look back at what had been her sanctuary for most of her pregnancy.

"You made it." Brother Evan greeted as he opened the back door of a secretive butcher shop. "Come inside." He lit a lamp and helped her through the door. He drew Amaya in a romantic embrace and lifted her face to his. In a deep kiss, he sucked on her tongue with his lips before releasing her.

"Yes, at last." Amaya panted and ignored the cramping low in her belly. It had been acting up for days. "Did you get it?"

"Of course, this way." They passed the empty slab tables and entered a small storage room. He lifted a stack of linens to reveal a small package filled with opium. As Amaya grabbed a special lantern from her satchel, she couldn't believe her luck.

Weeks after she arrived in London, Jacob allowed her to run errands to get acclimated to the city. This included running to the very butcher shop, where Evan now prepared their illicit drug through the lamp.

From the very first visit to the shop, Amaya overheard Asian folk talking about their secret shipments. In a gutsy move, she approached a Chinese gentleman leaving out the back door.

"You have something I might like?" She cooed in broken Mandarin.

"Hmmph. Perhaps?"

Amaya gathered the money Jacob had given her for errands. "I can get much, much more, I assure you."

The man squinted. "I don't deal with small ones like you."

"But sir, it is just for one. I am not competition, I assure you."

The stranger was very wary of this girl. She was Japanese, yet knew a smattering of mandarin, and knew he had the poppies. But money was money.

"I give you a sample for today. You like, I have more for you on Friday. Bring enough money, it will be good. Bring trouble to me, it will be death." He retrieved a small packet from his waistcoat and tossed it to Amaya.

Before she could speak, he was gone. Amaya came back on that Friday, and every Friday after that for just enough of the drug to help her relax. Her repeated visits drew the attention of the fishmonger who passed the butcher shop on the way to his booth at the market. This fishmonger knew a certain missionary that was looking for a Japanese girl like this one. For his inquisitive instincts, the fishmonger was paid well by Brother Evan.

But by the time Brother Evan had received word of Amaya's presence in London, the Japanese girl was very, very pregnant. A week before this night, Amaya's mysterious supplier did not meet her behind the butcher shop. Instead, it was Brother Evan who greeted her with a smile and a simple sentence that groomed Amaya for the taking. "I can get you plenty of this and help you escape this situation you're in."

Amaya had a weak heart for both the drug and Evan and agreed to meet again in one week.

They partook of the opium from the deceptive lantern. Evan made sure to intake the smallest amounts, for he needed to be completely conscious. Even as he smoked, he made plans to sell Amaya and her child to the insidious ones who'd already agreed to pay thousands for her back in Hong Kong. Tomorrow he would make the delivery. He just needed to obtain the right carriage.

"Well, my dear," Evan faked a deep inhale, "I must go. But rest here. I'll return before the dawn to take you with me."

"Hmm, anywhere but this place." Amaya cradled her belly as she slumped against the walls of a corner of the supply room.

"There's food and water in this basket." He shoved the container in her direction knowing full well that she would be too doped up to touch it. "See you in the morning, love." He shut the door.

Miles away, Jacob stirred in his sleep. The voice of a very small child awoke him. At first, he thought it was Amaya. But after a quick check of her empty room, he stumbled down the stairs in his dressing gown and peered into the shop. A small beam from a streetlamp outside beheld Amaya's doll, Fumi, face down on the floor. He picked it up and noticed that the fragile face had cracked.

"How did this happen?" A queer feeling came over him. Jacob threw on his coat and boots. He tried to prepare himself mentally for the worst.

Back at the butcher's shop, Amaya grasped at her belly. Even with the power of opium, she could feel the baby trying to push its way out. She was soaked in sweat and amniotic fluid.

Moments after Evan parted, the final contractions began. She'd ignored the initial signs that Jacob had warned her about, figuring it was more of his nonsense. Her eyes fluttered as she fought to stand and stay lucid. With her eyes closed, Amaya saw Fumi. The doll spoke to her. "Go home. Don't leave me."

"No. No. I can't go back." But a more severe contraction caused Amaya to double over.

"Home, go home." The voice was from a vision of her tiny toy, but it buzzed in her ears like a hive of bees.

"Yes, yes. Home." Amaya finally caved to the hallucinations and stumbled out into the street, just as Jacob came around the corner.

"Oh, papa, I've made a terrible mistake."

Jacob's heart burned, for Amaya called him by the name he'd wanted to hear. "I know, Amaya. Come, just a couple rows away."

Jacob used all his strength to get Amaya to Dr. Yoshito's shop. She grasped onto Jacob as pain racked her body. Once they arrived, Jacob pounded on the door. "It's time." He gushed when the doctor answered.

"Yes, let me help you." The kind doctor assisted them to his small kitchen behind the shop and called for his maid. "Let's set her on the floor." Once Amaya was on her back, Dr. Yoshito popped up to gather herbs, boil water, and grab blankets. The maid prepared for the baby's arrival at Amaya's feet.

As Amaya groaned, Jacob wiped her brow. "Breathe deep, long deep breaths."

Dr. Yoshito returned with his doctor bag and ginger root. "Help her chew this."

"Ahh, East meets West." Jacob held the root to her lips. "Amaya, this will help."

Amaya closed her eyes and put the plant to her lips. She squinted and grunted as she endured another contraction.

"It should be just a few minutes more." Dr. Yoshito cast a worried look at his maid. She shook her head. "Amaya, on the next episode, you'll need to push." The doctor commanded.

Amaya stuttered. Her head was on fire and bright flashes pierced her vision. Then a searing heat burned through her legs as Chika was born. The maid scooped her up and bathed the baby girl as the two men tried to comfort Amaya.

But it was too late. Amaya trembled for a moment and expired.

Jacob cried as he held Amaya's hand which began to cool.

"It is for the best. You have this one now." Dr. Yoshito leaned towards the maid who swaddled the child. "Call her Chika. It means wise flower. She will grow with the gifts that her mother did not understand."

Jacob covered Amaya's head. As he stood to gather Chika, Fumi fell from his waistcoat and landed on Amaya's belly. Fumi's fragile face was cracked in two.

An hour later, Jacob wrapped Fumi in a black cloth and set it next to Amaya's lifeless body in a small wooden coffin.

"I'm sorry, Sir, we need to go. It'll be light in a couple of hours." One of the Society men tapped Jacob on the shoulder.

"I need to go with her. It's tradition."

"Of course, Sir." The footman and driver lifted the coffin outside and onto a waiting carriage. Then they helped the broken cobbler up aside it. They retreated through the very early morning hours to the Thames. Jacob cried as he stroked the heavy wood of her eternal bed.

An hour later, Jacob, Dr. Yoshito, and a group of Society men sent Amaya on her journey in the afterlife. They stood on a deserted wharf at the edge of the Thames. Chika cried in the background as if she knew her mother was not coming back. The nanny cooed to her as she took the child away to be nursed.

As Amaya's purposefully weighted coffin sank into the Thames, Jacob whispered, "Goodnight my darling, Amaya. Fumi is there for you."

Across London town, a serious Discussion about the fate of Amaya was had.

"The visionary is dead? And her child taken by the Society?" A wealthy and powerful man, protected by shadows in a darkened room, lit a cigarette. The flame from his lighter and the red embers of the fag illuminated a red angry face.

"Yes, Sir." Brother Evan trembled. He'd completely blown

his mission by miscalculating Amaya's labor. He deserted Amaya thinking that he would have enough time to satisfy his desires in a bordello that was just a short bike ride away. Women were both Brother Evan's greatest weakness and best strength. He knew exactly how to seduce the naïve but couldn't seem to control his manly urges at the most inopportune times. Even money from two warring underground factions couldn't keep him away from the ladies. He paid the whore who serviced him with opium, and she was eager to share it with him. By the time Brother Evan burst into the butcher's shop, an angry washwoman was cleaning up the mess. The butcher had already reported his failure to Brother Evan's superior, a German man that he only knew as Mr. Gustav.

Mr. Gustav was now sneering at the Brother through the darkness. "And you dipped into our supply again, did you not?"

"I did, Sir." Evan knew that lying was pointless.

"Well, at least you are honest. I've never liked a liar." Wispy tendrils of smoke from Gustav's cigarette tickled Evan's nose. "You were supposed to have the girl and the child. Now we have neither."

"I know, but—"

"Sit down and shut up." Gustav flicked a flurry of ashes from his fag that fell like shooting stars onto his desk. "You do know that you overdosed Amaya and she perished?"

Brother Evan plopped into a plush velvet chair and grasped its sides. "I—I did not." His blanched face told another truth to his superior. Despite his penchant to pander to all kinds of women, Evan did still have feelings for Amaya. He was certain that the child she bore was his. Even in the darkened room, Mr. Gustav could see the shock.

"Pity. So now, we have nothing. Years of searching and infiltration wasted." Gustav coughed and seethed another drag. "You know what your punishment should be, do you not?"

"Yes. Death, Sir." Brother Evan prepared for the worst.

"More elimination of lives would not help this situation. And your seduction talents are still needed, especially with ladies and gentlemen of the cloth. I want you to return to the convent in Hong Kong as if you've just stepped off from a faux mission to Africa. You will need to act as if you know nothing of Amaya's absence and demise. I will send the next mission to you via our usual contact. Now get out." Gustav hissed.

Brother Evan scurried into the night. A couple of days later he promptly checked into the convent with small gifts for Mother Superior Agnes. "These are delightful!" She admired a pair of wooden native flutes. "Welcome home, Brother Evan!"

"Thank you, Mother Agnes." He bowed and kissed her ring.

"Sister Evie, prepare the usual room for Brother Evan." The Mother waved her hand to a stunning sister he'd never seen before. Sister Evie was a young pale Chinese woman with shimmering brown eyes with flecks of green.

"Come." The attractive young nun led the spy down two long corridors. After proffering a key from her pocket, the sister opened a sturdy wooden door with a creak. "In here." Sister Evie smiled.

Brother Evan set down his bag, sat on the sparse bed, and prepared to unpack. But Evie had other ideas. With a wicked grin, the comely sister closed the door behind.

"Would you like a drink? A little tipple?" Evie whisked a

leather sheathed flask from her robes and handed it to the Brother. Suddenly he was thirsty for more than the forbidden alcohol.

"Yes, why yes." He stuttered and swilled eagerly. "Delicious."

Sister Evie's eyes never left his as she removed her habit to reveal a freshly shaved head. "Please, enjoy more." Evie began to untie her belt.

The idea of having a fresh virgin nun titillated Evan. It would be the last thought he would have. The room swirled, blanketed to a misty haze, and then finally darkness as he expired from the poisoned drink.

Distracted by the last several day events, an opium hangover, and now a tainted taste of brandy and a nun's flirtations, Brother Evan hadn't noticed that Evie was the whore he'd been carousing with in London while Amaya perished.

Sister Evie flipped her robe inside out to reveal its grey woolen cloak side. She wrapped her headgear into a sleek-looking turban, exited the room, and headed straight for the foyer where Mother Agnes was waiting.

"It is done." Evie dipped out into the night as Mother Agnes sent word for an undertaker.

London, 1855

Nettie Singleton grinned as her mother dosed the light. Her fingers clutched a beautiful Japanese doll.

"Good night, mummy."

The Kicho

"Good night, dear." Her mother, Mrs. Dardin, parted with a wicked smile. She'd been able to procure the doll for a decent sum. More than she wanted to pay, but attainable. Nothing was too good for her only child. Nettie was quite spoiled.

Days before, while Mrs. Dardin was taking Nettie to singing lessons, the rotten mother spotted the gorgeous toy in the arms of a smaller child. As they departed from their carriage, Mrs. Dardin was already plotting. Before she could say anything about the striking doll, Nettie laughed.

"Mummy! Look at that."

"Yes, I see." Mrs. Dardin gazed at a charming Asian girl.

The foreigner appeared to be no more than five. She sat on a curb outside a cobbler's shop whilst running her fingers through the hard-to-obtain locks of the doll.

"It's beautiful." Nettie started to pull away from her mother.

"Wait, you can't be seen talking to her. I'll explain later. But do you want that doll?" Mrs. Dardin had never seen anything like it. And if Nettie wanted it, Mrs. Dardin would get it for her.

"Yes, mummy. Please. Pretty please with sugar on top."

"Stay right here at this bench. Don't move." Mrs. Dardin commanded. The determined mother gave a wary eye to her surroundings and then approached the young Japanese girl.

"Well, hello, love. That is quite the doll you have there." Mrs. Dardin's voice dripped with sugary sweet promise.

"Hello." Chika was startled from her play with the precious doll. "Thank you very, very much."

"May I hold your doll? Just for a moment?"

Chika paused. Her grandfather's warning echoed in her head. *Do not ever lose your dolly. Ever.*

"I'm ever so sorry Ma'am...but she's very special."

"Of course, I see. Well, I suppose she's in good hands then." Mrs. Dardin sneered and trudged to her daughter before Chika could answer. The wicked woman made note of the cobbler's address and gathered up Nettie for her lessons.

Chika's tummy tightened with worry as she held Aika closer. She would have to tell her grandfather about the strange woman.

After they arrived home, Mrs. Dardin urged Nettie into the house. "Go on in darling, I'll be in momentarily." The evil mother sniveled to the coachman. "You know of people who can grant favors?"

"Madam?"

"I need you to find someone to do a favor for me. You understand?"

"I believe I know a person, Madam. At the market."

"And the market is still open?"

"Yes, Madam."

"Take me there, now." Mrs. Dardin didn't wait for the coachman to help her into the carriage.

Within the half-hour, the coachman pointed out a fishmonger. "There, Madam, that man."

The Kicho

"Very good." Mrs. Dardin trotted off to the fish stall and approached the deviant fish dealer.

"You. I heard that you could do things. Special favors for money." Mrs. Dardin opened her pocketbook and showed the fishmonger a large stack of bills.

"Ah yes, Madam. Surely you have something in mind?"

"The girl that lives in the cobbler's house. One like, um, your people." Mrs. Dardin blathered.

"Yes, Madam?"

"She has a doll. It looks, well, like her. I want you to procure that doll. Do whatever necessary."

"Done. Come back here tomorrow about this time. I will have it for you." He promised as greed filled his soul and the strange lady's money lined his pocket.

That night as Chika prepared for a bath, she placed Aika on her bed next to an open window. The fishmonger couldn't believe his luck. With a simple reach, the prized doll was in his possession. By Nettie's bedtime the next eve, Mrs. Dardin presented Nettie with the fantastic doll.

"Good night, my darling."

"Good night, mummy."

Neighborhoods away, Chika cried in the arms of her grandfather until she finally fell asleep with exhaustion. Jacob worried that the strange lady that had approached Chika had wanted more than just her doll.

A few weeks later, the Dardin household was not as happy as it had been before.

"Nettie darling, please don't shake your dolly so hard." Mrs. Dardin rubbed her eyes. The clatter inside the new toy was giving her uncontrollable pain. And she swore it squeaked out petite, queer phrases. Mrs. Dardin ignored her imagination. "Nettie, bring her here."

"Yes, mummy."

After a thorough examination, Mrs. Dardin pressed the brass button on the doll's back, a small compartment opened, and a gold crown piece rolled onto the floor. "What's this? Did you know this was there?"

"No, mummy."

Mrs. Dardin adjusted the doll's clothing. "You can have her back. Go out and play then." As Nettie headed outside with the doll Mrs. Dardin swore, she heard a voice.

"Not mine."

She rubbed her ears. Surely, she was hearing things.

The next day Mrs. Dardin was determined to get value from the unique coin.

"That's not currency." A shopkeeper peeped over his glasses. "Never seen anything like that. You'll need to take it to the bank." He paused with a confident smile. "The Brooks Bank around the corner deals in foreign coinage. I'm sure they'll be able to help. Tell them Mr. Rigby sent you. Is this all then?" The shopkeeper wrapped up pricey candies for Mrs. Dardin who tried to pay for her items with the crown from the doll.

The Kicho

"Yes, thanks." Mrs. Dardin snatched up the special crown and dropped other money on the counter. "Keep the change." And as was her way, she trotted away without a word and headed straight for the Brooks Bank despite a nagging headache and grogginess.

Mrs. Dardin hadn't been sleeping well as of late. She was having odd dreams that Nettie's new doll was speaking to her. *Nonsense*, she mused as she entered the bank. Her vision seemed to double as she signed in with the clerk. It seemed to be forever before a banker called her to his desk.

"Thank you for seeing me. I don't have an account here, but a shopkeeper, Mr. Rigby, referred me to your establishment. I have this coin." She set the crown on the desk.

The banker was at the fullest attention for he knew that the woman before him was not the proper owner of the coin. "Mr. Rigby? Delightful gentleman. Ahh, and this?"

"Well, I found this coin. I have not a clue what it is for."

"Yes." The banker pretended to check the crown and prepared his words carefully. "I'm sorry to be the bearer of bad news, but this coin is worthless. Less reputable toy manufacturers put them in their toys as an added value. It is nothing but a cheap reproduction of good English money."

"What?" Mrs. Dardin grimaced. "What should I do with it?"

"Well, it may become valuable years from now, as a sort of relic, as long as you have the toy with it. Did you have the toy?"

"No," she lied, "I found this in the street. I'll just give it to my child." Mrs. Dardin ran from the banker as she felt like her head would explode in pain.

"Very well, Madam. Good day." The banker pulled a sheet of paper from his desk and wrote down a series of numbers. One set was the coin's identification. The other numbers were the address of Dr. Yoshito. He crossed the room and whispered to the clerk. "Follow her. Then her address. Nothing more."

Over the coming weeks, Mrs. Dardin's obsession with the doll and its mysterious coin began to accelerate.

"The doll…it says weird things." Mrs. Dardin poured her second glass of sherry. The first one hadn't even taken the edge off of her pain. Nettie had just gone to bed, and the Dardins were enjoying spirits in their parlor.

Mr. Dardin seriously questioned his wife's sanity. She'd been mumbling in her sleep. During the day, she yelled at the staff so severely that all but the cook had quit, and she would only work during the day. Mrs. Dardin's reputation was so repugnant that hiring new staff had been impossible.

"Well, dear, perhaps you need more rest? A holiday?" Mr. Dardin tried to cheer.

"Perhaps you should shut up." Mrs. Dardin threw her drink into the fireplace, glass and all. The flames hissed with the temporary addition of liquid fuel. "I'm going to bed. You can sleep down here, bastard."

Mr. Dardin cowered in his chair as the Mrs. stumbled up the stairs.

The next day, Mrs. Dardin slipped along the rain-slicked cobblestones. She had to find the fishmonger. She was certain he'd put a curse on the doll. If she could pay him enough, surely, he'd end the spell and her raging headaches would stop, she'd reasoned with herself. Even as she hustled to reach the market before closing, her head pounded terribly. She blinked through the fog and mist to see a young man at the fish stand pulling the last salmon off the trough and plopping it into a crate.

"You. You-hoo!" Mrs. Dardin squeaked breathlessly as she reached the corner booth. "You there. Hello, um, where is your, um. Well, I mean, is the other gentleman here today?"

The young Japanese man stood and squinted at the persistent woman before him. He didn't like rudeness, especially at closing time. "You are not here for fish? I have one salmon, that is all."

"No, no. I don't need a fish. I'm looking for—"

"No fish. No time for chit chat."

In desperation, Mrs. Dardin again opened her pocketbook while fumbling with her umbrella. "I have money for your time."

The new fishmonger stopped and looked around before he spoke. The suspicion in his gut rumbled worse than hunger pangs. "Be quick." He snatched the stack of bills she held out.

"Your friend, or the owner of the stall. Is he here today? Or tomorrow? I need to speak to him as soon as possible."

The fishmonger paled. "He is gone. Never come back."

"Whatever do you mean? You people are just—" Mrs. Dardin raised her voice in a panic.

"He died. Fell on street and crack head open. Like fragile egg. Die two days later." He hissed in broken English as he threw the cash back at the troublesome woman. She was very eager to pay for something he didn't have. The fishmonger rightly assumed that she'd done the same with his predecessor. It was time to be rid of her. "I close now. Sorry, I no help." He began to pull down the canvas flap over the merchandise.

"You knew him?" Mrs. Dardin stuttered.

"No, Ma'am. He die, no family. I get offer to work; I take it. Now I must go." He released the cord on the canvas, and it slapped shut in front of the woman.

"Hmmph." Mrs. Dardin rubbed her temples. She had no idea of how she'd get rid of her headaches now.

The new fishmonger vacated the market in the approaching nightfall. The fate of the previous fishmonger had been more complicated than he'd relayed to the strange woman. She would never find out that the man she'd hired to steal the doll had interrupted a very serious chain of events and was killed in a planned accident for the theft.

Hours later, Mrs. Dardin moaned in agony. She felt as if her head would split in two. The headaches didn't stop. Not for a single second since she'd been to the market. She'd tried all the medications the doctor had given her, but they only made the pain worse. She paced in front of the fireplace furiously rubbing her neck and forehead. With stiffened fingers, she yanked apart the lacing of her collar and dug her fingers into her neck.

"Mummy, will you read me a story?" Nettie whispered.

"You stupid, spoiled bitch! Read it yourself. You're old enough now. And you can get rid of that stupid doll." Mrs. Dardin moved toward her daughter, lost her balance, and fell to the floor on her side in a heap of tears.

Her husband jumped up from the lounger. "Nettie, go upstairs."

The Kicho

"But papa!"

"Just go Nettie. I'll be up in a little while to read to you." Mr. Dardin tried to remain calm despite the fact that he too was starting to experience horrific headaches. He bent over his sullen spouse and reached for her elbow. "Let me help you up, dear."

"Don't touch me." She shrieked as she scrambled to the staircase railing. She clawed her way to a standing position as Mr. Dardin shrugged.

"All right then dear, let me make tea."

"You do that." She leaned over the rail as again the voice of the doll repeated incessantly in her head. *You are not my Mummy.*

The room spun as Mrs. Dardin clung to the stairs. A piercing squeal sent waves of nausea and chills through her body. She stumbled over to the fireplace for warmth.

In the kitchen, Mr. Dardin shut off the whistling tea kettle and poured a cup for his ailing wife. As he added liberal amounts of sugar and milk, he wondered if she ever would be well again. He set a perfect tray with her favorite pot, matching cups, and a couple of flowers from a vase in the kitchen, in the hopes that their beauty would distract her. He rushed into the parlor, "My darling—"

"Stop that intrepid, god-forsaken noise you bloody fool!" Mrs. Dardin, in an insane rage, grabbed the hearth poker and like a well-trained fencer, stabbed her husband right through his middle. A scarlet patch of blood-soaked his waistcoat as the tea set crashed to the floor. Mr. Dardin fell backward with a grunt as Mrs. Dardin withdrew the poker with a grotesque pop. A last gasp escaped his lips as he expired.

The room was eerily quiet for a couple of seconds. The thuds of Nettie's sleepy footsteps broke the silence. "Mummy? Mummy, what happened? Where's papa?"

Mrs. Dardin glanced up from her horrific handiwork to see her daughter and the dreaded doll. *You are not my Mummy. You are not my Mummy.* The tiny voice persisted in Mrs. Dardin's head.

"Nettie, close your eyes, don't look." With one quick slash, Mrs. Dardin cut her throat open with the poker and collapsed on the floor.

Nettie screamed and bolted outside in her nightdress towards the next-door neighbor. As she hurried away, the doll fell amongst shrubbery and into the dewy evening grass. The constable was called and the Dardin household was hastily cordoned off. Within hours, peace had enveloped the stately homes of the block.

A lone man strolled through the misty eve and stopped in front of the Dardin household. With only silent streets as his witness, the new fishmonger picked up the treasured doll and gently tucked it into his heavy woolen cloak. Aika would be returned to her rightful owner.

The next day, Nettie was allowed back in the house to collect scant belongings under the direction of a dour-looking nun. Soon she would join the orphan's home. She was able to keep just one toy and it wasn't a doll.

The next eve, Jacob tucked Chika tightly into her bed with Aika at her side, her coin inside her belly. "Well now, isn't that better?"

"Yes, grandfather."

"Chika will always be yours now, to make you feel

protected." Jacob patted the toy.

"But grandfather, I've always been protected." Chika hugged her dolly.

"Whatever do you mean, Chika?"

"While Aika was gone, her mummy Fumi came at night to keep me company. She assured me that Aika would be back." Chika enthused.

"I see. Well, that's wonderful news. Good night, and you can tell me more in the morning." Jacob ignored the goosebumps on his skin. He learned long ago not to question the wisdom of the dolls.

The Dolls of Society Series will continue.

ABOUT THE AUTHOR

Victoria L. Szulc is a multi-media artist and author. Victoria's work has been recognized in St. Louis Magazine (2019 A-List Reader's Choice Author 2nd Place winner), Amazon UK Storytellers 2017 semi-finalist, the Museum of the Dog, and her illustrations of Cecilia for "Cecilia's Tale" won a runners up award for The Distinctive Cat Stephen Memorial Award 2019.

Inspired by the works of Beatrix Potter, the Bronte sisters, Jane Austen, C.S. Lewis, and Ian Fleming, she "lives" her art through various hobbies including: drawing, writing, volunteering for animal charities, yoga, voice over work, and weather spotting. She specializes in pet portraiture through her company The Haute Hen.

For character development she's currently learning/researching chess, fencing and whip cracking. Victoria blogs about these adventures at: mysteampunkproject.wordpress.com

and

https://haute-hen-countess.square.site/

"Adventures abound and romance is to be had."

-*Victoria*

BOOKS FROM VICTORIA L. SZULC

More works (and future releases) by Victoria L. Szulc:

The Society Trilogy (a steampunk series, revised):
Book 1-Strax and the Widow
Book 2-Revenge and Machinery
Book 3-From Lafayette to London

More Society Steampunk Stories (revised):
A Long Reign, The Society Travelers Series, v.1
The Kicho, The Dolls of Society, v.1
A Dream of Emerald Skies, A Young Society Series, v.1

The Brown Lady, Short Story Edition

The Vampire's Little Black Book Series (revised): v. 1-15

The Vermilion Countess Series

A Book of Sleepy Dogs

Made in the USA
Monee, IL
27 August 2022